Happy Holidays to you!

Thank you so much for being a part of my Goodreads Giveaway for ***Collard County***! The peculiar citizens of Collard County look forward to meeting you!

I am delighted that you chose my book as an entry!

Enclosed you will find an autograph copy of your book. I welcome your reviews and reflections on Goodreads and on Amazon! The book is also available on various electronic devices!

If you like what you read, PLEASE SHARE IT !

I invite you to visit my home on the web at www.tamarajmadison.com for updates on new releases, writing resources, and my blog, TamTalk!!! Feel free to share your comments there as well.

Thanks for having a passion for literature and supporting it. I look forward to hearing from you!

Tamara J. Madison

Collard County

a collection of short stories

Tamara J. Madison

ISBN:
ISBN-13: 978-1492926078
ISBN-10: 1492926078

ALSO BY TAMARA J. MADISON

Kentucky Curdled, poetry and essay
https://www.createspace.com/4456625

Kentucky Curdled, poetry audiobook
www.cdbaby.com/tamarajmadison

Naked Voice (spoken word recording
www.cdbaby.com/tms

TamTalk!!! (bi-monthly newsletter)
www.tamarajmadison.com

For the author's blog, updates, happenings, and latest releases, go to www.tamarajmadison.com.

DEDICATION

For Adrienne,
thanks for that push that only you know how to give me.

CONTENTS

ACKNOWLEDGMENTS

Many thanks to the following literary magazines who graciously dared to publish these stories:

Catalyst Literary Journal

Kola

Rockford Kingsley, Ltd.

Tea Party Magazine

Warpland

I also wish to acknowledge the women writers' retreat of **Hedgebrook**, http://www.hedgebrook.org, where these stories were first drafted. My stay at Hedgebrook was healing, unforgettable and necessary for my growth as a writer.

†

My heartfelt thanks also to the many fans and followers who have loved these stories for years and have persistently encouraged me to publish them and share their magic with others.

PREFACE

I am a poet baptized in the rhythm, melody and imagery of my familial and cultural ancestry. These stories are purposely dense, visual and rhythmically driven like poetry. Rather than call them "short stories," I prefer to call them "poetic fiction," or better yet, "poetic paranormal." I pray that you are inspired and intrigued by the adventure!

Be Joyful,
Be Creative,
Be Inspired!

Tamara

BARREN

Thus named to reflect the history of the land, Indigo County was really no more than a town, but the pompous residents in command insisted on the privileges and prestige of a "county." The town's name murmured of its centuries of growth from the great indigo plantations tilled and toiled by the funk of free labor. With the Emancipation and Lee's Surrender long since passed, East Indigo's prominent citizens remained rich off the wealth from former slave hands and bustled about their business in rainbow hues of blue starched and pressed to arrogant perfection. Colored folks from West Indigo, however, existed on snatches of laughter and joy barely breathing through their dull, tattered, color limp rags. Many still bore stained hands as constant reminders of the degradation that had festered their humanity.

West Indigoers were not to be seen in East Indigo before the sun raised its head or as it closed its eyes. Many a colored body had drug from wagons, waved in the wind from whimpering trees or raced as supper from hungry hounds if caught in East Indigo at the wrong time, in the wrong place, by the wrong persons. With the so-called outlaw of slavery, East Indigoers carefully established colored quarters, boundaries and regulations and meticulously enforced them. All heaven help a colored stranger stumbling into town unaware.

Rumor ran that the reason indigo and other crops grew so well in this place was because of all the "nigra" blood and flesh that had fertilized the soil. Prosperous farmers joked and teased that "'nigra' blood could make dung and ashes sprout fruit and flowers in the desert." None of them seemed to mind at all as long as a few "nigra's" remained to till and plant and feed the gluttonous prosperity of East Indigo.

Well, times had long since changed in many ways and the Mayor of East Indigo bustled about with that change. With his inheritance as a play field, he grew to be a big man with big plans, needing big, big plots of land to develop those plans with commerce as the key to continued financial success. North, east and south of East Indigo were white settlements and already developing projects. The only place to move was across the tracks.

The Mayor and his "special affairs" council had exhausted their tactics to scare West Indigo away. Apparently the coloreds had adapted to burning crosses and threats and paid them no more mind than dust under bushes. Though the Mayor and his council had plenty of gruesome ideas left, some of the coloreds would still be needed to clean their toilets and provide amusement, thus care must be taken not to rid the town of all of them. With the swelling of his dreams, the Mayor grew restless and desperate to scoot the coloreds away from those tracks. The railroad would be vital for business. Foreseeing no other alternative, many of the coloreds just had to be removed.

After many months of the Mayor's unsuccessful efforts, the perfect opportunity rode into town in government cars. City- slick officials donning dark suits, stepping quickly in shiny shoes, flashing badges, and clutching secret files, spoke big words with vapid breath and no melody in their mouths. Only their lips moved when speaking; the rest of their faces, framed with dark plastic shields concealing their eyes, remained frozen and numb like their spines.

Indigo, "a highly recommended, domestic candidate," had been invited to participate in a "medical experiment" due to lack of funding to carry the mission overseas. With a greedy go ahead from the Mayor, a "free clinic" with a "doctor" and a "nurse" along with all the "necessary equipment and paraphernalia" were positioned at the railroad tracks, of course, in West Indigo. After thanking the Mayor for contributing to this "research in modern medicine," the men road away as swiftly and surreptitiously as they had come, tediously wiping away every speck of their presence. Pockets plumped and restlessness subdued, the Mayor sat fat and waited.

Mysteriously only a couple of weeks stood between the day of the "clinic" installation and the day of the rumbling steel birds that flew over West Indigo. No one solicited the services of the "free clinic" for those standing weeks between. The white building housing the white "doctor" and white "nurse" clad in bleach white uniforms with their shiny, sharp surgical instruments did not at all appeal to West Indigoers. Luttie Belle May Hawk Richardson III had healed their ailments since anyone could remember.

Luttie Belle May was an old knot-looking woman even when she stood straight and tall. She had been a pretty "yaller gal" once with the kind of long, wavy, raven hair that made men drool. Now adorned with eagle feathers and shells, her hair still hung long but had not been combed folks figured since before the war, and it looked as though some kind of creature just might live in that nest of nappiness somewhere.

Luttie Belle May hardly spoke or visited folks. She tended her garden of collard greens and roots and formulated her potions to be ready for the many troubled souls that knocked upon her door. Some say she looked like such a knot because she laid hands on folks and absorbed their pain, bore it upon herself, carried it for them. Luttie Belle May was the most respected, most feared soul in town, east or west. Council meetings, town gatherings, holidays, births, the joining of lives, and deaths in West Indigo held Luttie Belle May at the helm of all their affairs. She rarely uttered a word, but when she did, ears fell upon their knees and humbled themselves to listen. Luttie Belle May's house and garden stood as sentinel right near the railroad tracks directly behind the new clinic.

The rumbling steel birds dove and soared above West Indigo in great display. A sticky, wet, foul smelling substance sprayed from their bellies settling onto rooftops, smothering gardens, muffling whispering flowerbeds and drowning gurgling wells. Luttie Belle May knew of their coming and began hastily making preparations while the Mayor stood safely on his porch watching with a grimy grin, fondling coins in his pockets.

Within a few days, every man, woman, and child had fallen suspiciously ill and desperately searched for some type of treatment. When Luttie Belle May's prescriptions failed them, West Indigoers, against her caution, flocked to "the clinic" for their deliverance. After all times had changed and Luttie Belle May was getting old; maybe she just wasn't mixing properly these days. Men, elders and children were restricted to visiting the clinic on Mondays and Wednesdays. Women, ages 15-50, were seen throughout the rest of the week except Sunday. The men recovered from the dry coughing, burning rash, bubbling blisters and bleeding noses rather quickly with a few injections and a dose or two of medicine. The women's wounds, however, did not heal so easily...

Fearful and confused by the fits from their own bodies, the women piled into the clinic where they were herded into corners, draped behind an uncaring curtain, and thrust rapidly out the door. The waiting room convulsed from their nauseating presence. Some of the women held hands; others dabbed stinging tears and profusely bleeding noses. All sat with knees glued together praying that the river rushing from their erupting wombs would suddenly, miraculously halt.

Sharp pains ricocheted from the tips of their breasts to the lips of their enlarged labia leaving their swollen insides exhausted from battle.

Mothers, daughters, grandmothers, sisters, and aunts avoided the horror and helplessness in one another's eyes. They questioned themselves searching for answers and reasons for the life dripping tortuously from their bodies. Like they had closed themselves customarily during their moons, they now shamefully hid themselves from their fathers, husbands and sons suffering alone the heinous curse.

"Next" is simply how and what the women were called. To the "doctor" and "nurse" at the clinic, they remained nameless, faceless and oblivious to anything human or even life-like. When summoned, each womanly eased herself from the bench and dragged herself helplessly behind the blood stained curtain.

"Strip from the waist down. Lie quietly. Feet in the stirrups." These next commands did not contain the slightest hint of compassion or skill in bedside manner. Feverishly each woman followed instructions without hesitation relinquishing the hope of any other alternative.

In the beginning, the staff had cleaned and sterilized the instruments according to professional procedure. After monotonous hours of the same operation over and over again, the "doctor" replaced the necessity of procedure, sterility, or even cleanliness with the selfish demand of convenience. One by one, he slashed the women from their breastplate to their pubic bone often with stained instruments barely even rinsed. The "doctor" plowed stubbornly through their bodies ripping, tearing, and cutting selfishly to find evidence in support of his "experiments." A black-eyed, full moon howled as screeching tears crashed against the linoleum. Shocked tubes, ovaries, and uteri splattered and shuddered against the cold, clammy porcelain of the nearby sink.

Like patching a piece of ragged dungarees, the "doctor" sewed them back together. He had divorced himself from the inhumane cruelty of this "duty", this "work" long before even arriving in Indigo. Someday the world would thank him for his brave research and ingenious discovery in "modern medicine." These "specimens" were merely contributing to the saving of millions of lives in the very near future, lives like his two charming daughters and lovely young wife.

After significant analysis and recording, the staff disposed of the remains of their research by dumping them in a covered earthen pit behind the "clinic." From a short distance, Luttie Belle May observed and shuddered hearing the earth moan and feeling it shift in great anguish beneath her feet. For three days and three nights in a smoke filled house, she fasted and prayed, fasted and prayed, fasted and prayed for her people.

When the "clinic" closed for two weeks on vacation and left no one in its care, Luttie Belle May diligently put the results of her own "research" to work. She sat loyally at the bedside of every woman who died after lying beneath the “doctor's” knife. Some of the women did recover, however, and Luttie Belle May nursed them as she had always done in the past. None of the women or their families ever returned to the "clinic."

In the dead of winter, Luttie Belle May plowed the rock-frozen, ground and planted. Blood boiling in her veins, she worked arduously neatly establishing rows, cradling the seeds in her hand and blessing each one before softly burying them in the earth. Daily she tended them, watered and weeded them singing all the very while. Folks in West Indigo passed by smiling; this must truly be a good sign baring the news of desperately needed good times. Luttie Belle May never ever sang before.

In due season with powerful prayers, tender tending, and the breath from the Creator's own lips, the seeds took root and unfurled beneath the ground. Swaddled in lush collard green leaves, the seeds all grew anxiously to full term. This time, the earth shifted in the pain of labor and joy of birth as warm rains showered happily all over West Indigo. Neighbors in East Indigo stood in their yards staring in disbelief at the bright clouds bursting rainbow-tinted diamonds over the little shantytown. For months the fields and landscapes of East Indigo had suffered drought and still no rain came to their side of the tracks. "Must not be enough 'nigra' blood," though many while gazing upon their barren fields, shaking their heads not knowing how very wrong they were.

After meticulously counting moons, Luttie Belle May sent word that the women folk must gather in her garden for a special "healing ceremony" at midnight of the next new moon. Each woman was instructed to bring blankets and dress with protection from the pending heavy rains. The women began assembling at half past eleven. Curious and puzzled, all were in place by a quarter 'til the hour chattering and whispering, speculating as to why Luttie Belle May had requested them. Many wondered if she had grasp of her right mind, singing and carrying on like she had been lately.

On the sixth stroke of midnight, the skies again sprinkled sweet rain, and Luttie Belle May appeared on the front porch hobbling on her one good leg out to the yard where the women waited with swollen breasts and all sorts of questions spilling from the tips of their tongues. Luttie Belle May said nothing but fell on her knees and prayed a howling, melodic prayer in a strange tongue. The louder she prayed, the harder the rain fell as the clouds rode the waves of a warm, wet wind.

The women's eyes widened in amazement as the earth contracted beneath their feet causing most to drop to their knees. Still praying, Luttie Belle May greeted each woman by drizzling drops of oil in her palm and instructing her to massage the strangely clumped collards greens at her feet. Curiously the women all squatted and gently stroked the leaves with oil and rainwater. One by one, the leaves shifted to the music of the earth's moan.

Instinctively, each woman carefully pealed the leaves one after the other in growing anticipation. In the center of each clump lay a plump bundle (sometimes two) of love with clear, shining eyes, thick, dark, curly hair, toothless squeals, and fat feet kicking and flapping collard green leaves. Ecstatic with tear- soaked laughter and breasts overflowing, the mothers bundled their babies and pressed them close to the emptiness they had carried shamefully for so long. Each woman arose and kissed Luttie Belle May Hawk Richardson III as she blessed the child in her arms.

†

Upon discovering the tampering with and stolen evidence from the "pit of women's parts," the "clinic," its "nurse," and "doctor" abruptly disappeared from East Indigo. The Mayor panicked in disbelief and gross disappointment at the vastly growing population of coloreds in West Indigo. The "research" evidently had failed him. Why damn near all of them "nigra's" had babies. All the boys were named "Richard," "Richardson," or "Hawk," and "Luttie's," "Belle's," and "May's" just spilled all over everywhere. Convinced that his plans of expansion had failed, the Mayor fled angrily never asking questions. The city slick officials never reappeared for the results of their research and never ever would.

Even without the continuous violent spill of "nigra" blood, West Indigo so prospered that they just ran the East Indigoers out from even their own side of the railroad tracks. Within a decade colored folks, dressed like psychedelic peacocks in free flowing feathers flooded both sides of town, and commercial development proceeded under the palms of blue stained hands. Not a pale face could be found for miles. Incidentally, the town soon changed its name from East or West Indigo to Collard County.

MISPLACED

My last $9.00, tucked away in a bank envelope, the same $9.00 that has to last me at least a week. I am standing in the middle of the living room floor looking for it. I quickly search all the places where the envelope should be: the stack of bills whining to be paid, the pile of PTA flyers and bulletins screaming for my attention, and even the bulk of business correspondence continually gnawing at the knot in my stomach. But no last $9.00.

I tear up the bedroom, the kitchen, the kids' room, even the bathroom and finally return to the living room filled with my frustration. Something possesses me to go back through that clutter of papers. The perspiration of my fingertips stamps each page with anxiety as I frantically flip and scan again.

There it is right on the same shelf that I have looked over twice already, tucked between file folders. Now for a check list just to be sure: $9.00 in wallet, wallet in hand, keys in their usual place, cloth grocery sack on my arm, jacket wrapping my back, driver's license, stove off, answering machine on, note attached to the refrigerator door, and I'm ready. Ready to pick up the clothes from the cleaners, meet with a prospective client, grab the mail from the post office, search for poster board and molding clay for the children's school projects, and stop by the office to meet with my boss regarding the revision of my work schedule and conveniently, continually forgotten raise. Before I drop dead, I'll eventually make it to the market to pick up some fresh vegetables and bath salts.

Wallet, keys, license, grocery sack, jacket, brief case, $9.00... Something is still missing, and I am still standing in the same place in the middle of the living room floor. "Now where did I put **myself**?" These words creep into my consciousness, burst my soul's veins and then dance hauntingly about my living room. What kind of question is that to ask? "Where did I put **myself**?" I say the words aloud again, and they step mocking circles about me laughing at my confusion. Blood rushing and heart pounding, my feet anchor themselves in the carpet against my will, and I can no longer move. The clock hands freeze. The phone and doorbell refuse to ring. I watch my wallet, keys, license, grocery sack and jacket drop to the floor, yet I cannot hear them or feel them released from my fingers. I can no longer remember where I am going or what I am doing in the middle of the living room as I repeat those words, "Where did I put **myself**?"

My hands tremble as I stare at them in utter bewilderment. I have three finger nails and two whole fingers gone. Three of my natural nails have been stripped from the cuticle to the tip leaving soft, blackened flesh. Suddenly that knot in my stomach bursts; my insides begin to burn. The two whole missing fingers have left shiny scars like polished brass. Nothing is hurting, no blood, no pus, no torn tissues. Evidently the wounds aren't even scabbed and healed over quite some time ago.

The tremble of my hands has invaded the rest of my body including my feet now loosened from the carpet. My feet shuffle slowly as my body glides along slightly behind them; all of me lands before the full length mirror in the bedroom. Burning, numbness, missing fingers and nails. What else? Afraid to peel my gaze from the intricate wooden carvings along the mirror's frame, my insides convulse as my eyes stumble upon my reflection. Where is my nose? My right eye? My lobe of my ear on the same side? I stare in disbelief at the glazed stubs. The acidic burning of my insides swells, pounds in my chest and finally explodes from my face smacking against my reflection. My reflection bleeds the vomit of my anguish as the dense wreaking liquid slides from the mirror to drown my feet. The bitter residue stains the insides of my cheeks and dries like plaster at the corners of my mouth.

A thick trickle of sweat escapes the tension of my neck and rolls quickly down my back. My abdomen heaves. I fear whatever else is missing and how long it's been gone. Why didn't I notice before now? Sitting on my bed, I hardly remember removing my clothes scattered wildly about the room.

Again before the mirror, I examine my remaining eye. Dull and encased by heavy, dark circles, it glares back at me accusingly. Inhaling deeply, I can feel there is more, more of me missing like my missing eye, my liquid brown/almond eye, my eye that my grandfather gave me. It has lost its shine. Perhaps it would have been better to lose both of them and hide somewhat from the horror of it all. Unable to fully face my losses, I close my remaining eye and decide to let the palms of my hands do the seeing for me. Perhaps this will be easier. My hands find my hair still there, seemingly every single inch from the frizzy softness of the ends to the tight curls of my kitchen and all the stubborn strength in between. I cannot remember the last time I ran my fingers through my hair. I notice that it is thinner, just a bit thinner. Thin enough to make me aware of all my withering, falling apart piece by piece and not even knowing it.

Working their way south, my sweaty palms brush and dampen my forehead smoothing ashen lines that I have just discovered. Perhaps they have been there for years, and I never really wanted to see them. (Smile) Normally I would frown at wrinkles, think of them as a nuisance to the last lick of youth I have left, but now I am grateful for anything, any part of me that's left. My fingertips brush the hump of my remaining eye's lid and the limpness of the other one across from it. I miss my nose, broad and stubbornly arched with gentle, wide arcs on the sides. I always thought I wanted another one until now. My hands find my cheekbones holding up my jaws drooping just a bit. The corners of my mouth seem to have hardened over the years but ease with the warmth of a brief smile that soothes the churning of my insides.

My hands glide across a stubborn remnant where my chin used to be and then find my left ear still in place with my shoulders, neck and chest likewise. Gradually tears seep beneath my tightly closed eyelids as my palms cup the crude, hollow where my left breast used to be. My mind spins desperately searching for reason. Was it the greedy hands of some lover or a perverse advance from someone I passed on the street or met at work? Perhaps the last weary head that took residence on my breast just walked off with it. Did I even have it when I nursed my last child? What if it just up and left? It's a wonder both breasts are not gone. I always thought I'd feel less of a woman if I were to lose one. I thought I'd even die if I had to lose both. But for some reason, I feel more of a woman now than ever before.

Tired, worn, used, empty, hungry, tired. With tender touches, my palms slide from my aching shoulders to my elbows. Mph! Just what I need, elbows. What do I ever do with them? At an early age, I learned to never rest my weight upon them and use creams to keep them silken and smooth. Maybe that's why they remain because they have the luxury of simply being: round and hard, adorned with soft, scarred skin, a midpoint on the map of my frail arms. I treasure them now. They are a couple of the few things I don't have to miss. Like here... No navel with the mole to the left of it. The big, pretty, perfectly round, ink black mole that I never even considered as a beauty mark until now. Didn't I have a mole on my chin too?

Upon further inspection, my hands discover that whoever or whatever walked off with parts of me left my butt, hips and thighs intact. Like floor model TV's and stereos, they were probably too heavy to steal with the rest of my stuff. The thief got away with a knee, a few teeth, one of the knobs of my ankles, and a few toes too. I wonder what he would do with an injured knee that's needed surgery for the past two years or ankles that swell with too much pressure. Perhaps he's not as smart as he thinks he is. Maybe I'm not either. Was it really a man? Could one woman really do that to another? Did it all happened at one time, or did I disappear in pieces? Did someone or something really take me, or did I give **myself** away? As if this isn't enough... My palms graze between my thighs... My honey is missing, snatched from between my hips like a mangled petal from a flower!

No more blind discoveries; this I have to see. Snatching open my eyes, I bend over before the mirror peeling the mountainous flesh of my thighs to fit my head between my legs. I can't find my honey. It is gone! In a frenzy, I search under my arms, beneath my only breast, between the crook of my elbows and knee, even stand my hair all over my head and still can't find my honey. Now how could I miss that? After all, haven't I been taught, since the day I could walk, to protect it? "Keep your dress down!" "Close your legs!" "Cross your ankles, honey, not your knees!" All that training and worry of it ending up in the wrong hands, and I just up and lose mine!

I live in a house with four of the most curious children and one of the brightest men God ever created, and no one has noticed that I am one-eyed, clip eared, chinless, half breasted, navel/knee/vagina less, let alone all the missing fingers, teeth and toes. Don't I cook, clean, pacify, bandage, council, on a daily? And what about making love three times a week? With what? What is wrong with these people/my family? Nobody notices? What is wrong with me?

I picture myself featured in a world records' anthology, the tabloids and even a travelling freak show as one of the main attractions. Suddenly the ridiculousness of it all is simply too much to handle. I begin with a nervous chuckle and then end up rolling all over the bedroom carpet spilling over into howling laughter.

What else can I do but laugh? I realize and finally admit that I am not the victim of a violent crime or even an emotional assault. No one took me away or borrowed me without my permission. I've given myself away for years. Haven't I? Time after time, again and again and again. No one needed to notice because somehow I managed to keep on supplying the needs and wants of others, despite my losses. I feed, dry tears, and apply emotional bandages, sprinkle smiles of pride, and spoon encouragement with the least bit of a beckoning from my job to home to school to the club and back again. Why would anyone notice?

Belly aching with laughter, cheeks tight with tears, and face flushed, I no longer have the energy to be angry or even sad. How could I have been so ignorant and insensitive to my own needs and maintenance? How did I let it get this far for this long? Out of all the things I always remember for everyone and everything else, how could I forget about **myself**?

With a sudden spurt of energy, I bustle about the house in search of **myself** laughing and quite certain that no one will ever believe this if I choose to tell it. Emptying drawers, shuffling papers, cleaning closets, clearing cabinets, and rearranging furniture, I begin collecting **myself** again. I happen upon my left breast balled up and soiled behind the television in the living room. I rarely ever watch TV. That knee I have missing is neatly folded and hidden in the bathroom cabinet under the sink with the child-proof lock on the door where all the disinfectants are stored. A few fingers, toes, nails and teeth are found every place from the kids' rooms and behind the stove and refrigerator to other least suspecting corners of the house, corners that I can't even fit. Most of the pieces are well preserved, even functional; they just aren't attached to me. Some of them are a bit dusty or dirty and maybe a stain or two, but nothing at all a little Epsom salts, sweet smelling soaps, and loving won't heal.

After searching each room in the major part of the house, I decide to tackle the storage. I unlock an old cedar chest just to see what might be in it. Beneath the mildew from ages, I open the lid and sift through a number of faded photographs and yellowed handkerchiefs. Many of the items I don't even recognize. Finally I find a snow white, ruffled handkerchief tied by a wide, satin, ruby ribbon. I pick up the tiny bundle, untie it and hold my breath while unfolding the corners. Wrapped with lightly scented tissue is my right eye. Scarlet lines are etched along the ivory surface, the iris lifeless. Rocking my eye gently in my palms, I dab it with tears and the few smiles I have left as the sun's setting magenta pours through the window.

After endless hours in the attic, I return to the living room and gather the recently recovered parts of **myself.** I am sure that there are pieces scattered about the car and/or garage and maybe even all the way to work and a client's house. I imagine trying to explain **myself** to one of my clients, "Excuse me, but you haven't seen any severed toes or extra vaginas laying around your home have you?" Believe it or not, this time my laughter is sane, tender and warm. If I have to spend the rest of my life, I'll find the rest of **myself**. And though I know I'll never be the same, I shall put **myself** back together and be stronger even if a finger or knee never work as well as before...

Tears again, but these tears are mending tears laced with love for **myself** and anyone or anything that ever got a piece of me. These tears are for their having to do without me for a time while I heal and mend **myself** back together. These are tears of thanksgiving because I could have been abused by someone or something else besides my own ignorance and negligence. Tears. Last but not at all least, these tears are hope for the me I see in you tired, hungry, aching, misplaced.

CYCLES

"Go see Red!" Ma'Mari almost stammered to her daughter as the words trudged from the back of her throat, tripping helplessly from the tip of her tongue.

"Go see RED!" Ma'Mari spat her words this time with a tender insistence that Iona knew not to challenge.

For years Ma'Mari had listened in pained, girdled silence; listened to timely tales and viatic visions; listened to her child reveal the secrets of secrets clawing behind the sealed rubbery gums of the town's elders. Ma'Mari listened to her daughter as a toddler coo contentedly alone in corners of the house playing with the spirits themselves. Ma'Mari could not see them, but she knew they made merry all about her home whenever they so willed, and she knew they made themselves known to her child.

Iona, Ma'Mari's third and last baby, gasped for her first breath of life beneath a crimson veil cloaking her face. Gently, silently she came into the world, after 36 hours of tortuous labor, seemingly knowing that there would be plenty of time for screaming tears later. Ma'Mari soon after drew her child birthing years to a close, not wanting to press her luck any further. Nine babies miscarried between the second child and her last. Ma'Mari carried each one just a little longer than the one before it. Each time she mourned more cradling the tiny remains in her hands before Red eased them away. Ma'Mari then wrapped her arms about herself as far as she could and squeezed to soothe the ache from the tiny tomb carved in her womb. Blessing every internment with her secret smile, Red buried the bleeding seeds in the burning earth at midnight, side by side, time after time, on the highest hill in the country, anticipating the great harvest.

"Hey! Baby gal!" sang a skillet sizzling voice from across the street.

"Hi, Mr. Lewis," grinned Iona with a flood of twinkling teeth.

"Where you call yourself going on a beautiful day like today?" the elder called after Iona as she paused from her stroll down the road.

"Ma'Mari sent me to see Miss Red," she replied reluctantly.

A brief shadow brushed Mr. Lewis' face right beneath the brilliantly beaming sun. On this, the hottest day in July, a chill crept along the pricking sweat of the old man's neck. The elders, like Mr. Lewis, all called Iona an "ole folk's chile", even though her mother carried only 21 young years during the birth. Many claimed there was a powerful "telling" in the blood that coated her birth veil.

"Pay my respects to Miss Red. You heah'?" he responded, his heart whispering a prayer for the child and her calling.

As Iona gingerly approached the road to Red's house, she noticed the door wide open. Now Red always kept her house closed. Even in the smoldering, sultry summer's dew, all doors, windows, cracks and crevices were sealed shut. Everyone wondered why, but no one dared ask Red about anything let alone her doors. Iona hesitated. She had always loved to go to Red's house, though none of the other children were allowed, not even her own brother and sister. This time, however, like an ancient tree deep rooted, she stood motionless, almost afraid as the door awaited the usual youthful dance of her carefree steps.

"Go see RED!" Her mother's words echoed hauntingly. Ma'Mari had never said Red's name like that before. Was something wrong? She had simply told Ma'Mari about the last dream, about the snake-like dragon with pulsating humps throughout its huge, never ending body, sprinkled with dirt-red splotches. This thing chased her all about a huge mansion unlike any place she had ever seen or been. With all her might, she fought; unafraid she fought; though it killed many others that she didn't know who, she fought. Iona had grown accustomed to her lucid dreams. She always remembered them. She always told Ma'Mari. Ma'Mari had never commented until now, "Go see RED!"

Iona sat running her fingers through the grass at the lane's edge, her plump legs bathed in the cotton, rainbow bouquet of her sundress and the dust of the lane. Her shoulders, sun-kissed all summer long, suddenly began to burn.

Unexpectedly, Red appeared on the front porch. Without her saying a word, Iona heard her voice. Rising slowly she glided through the powdered blades that brushed her feet, memorizing each foot and toe print. She would never walk this path the same again...

No one knew how old Red was, and no one remembered her not being there. The town paid her the respect of being old enough to name "dirt's mammy." Time, nonetheless, refused to settle onto her cinnamon skin, though centuries huddled in her eyes. A cascade of frizzy, charcoal curls laced with silver sparks shimmied down her back to greet a tight waist clamped between broad shoulders and hammering hips. Strangely Red's hair danced even when wind and she herself stood still. Folks claimed that she was half Indian and that the rivers of

Africa dashed in her veins as well; thus the powers of the land had blessed her.

Though she delivered all the blessed bundles of life for the other women, those same powers snatched all her own babies before their breathing time. She, nevertheless, refused to bare the blunt and brand of an old maid, and men flew out of the wood work just to land at her knees. Folks assumed that she couldn't be "leashed" by a natural man. Rumors ran that her woman thang had killed more than one man or two, and they all died smiling. Regardless, when Red's presence interrupted the town's meetings, men folk would break out in grinning sweats, and trip over their own tongues while keeping hands and hats over their laps as Red tossed her womanishness about the room. Many a man slept in stiff, frozen beds with wintry women on these nights.

Thick smells of herbs, wood and womanhood wrapped about Iona's nose as she followed Red through the doorway. As always the room was comfortably dim and familiar except a long stretch of wall that always donned a curtain. On this day, the curtain, removed, revealed shelves upon shelves of glass jars-- fat jars, slender jars, tall jars, tiny jars-- all tightly sealed; all completely filled with a dense, dark liquid. Iona thought that she saw a bubble or two in one of the jars upon her first glance, but the authority in Red's voice quickly snatched her attention. "Never let your calling have to call you more than once, chile."

Iona dropped her head in shame knowing that she should not have lingered before Red's pathway. "Yes, ma'am," she muttered in response.

"'Tis a new day and shame don't become you, chile," the raspiness in Red's voice softened. "Mean what you do and do what you mean, no matter what the others say."

Iona's ears drank Red's words knowing she would never repeat herself with questions rarely (if ever) allowed. Iona realized that the "new day" of which Red had often spoken had finally come.

"Ma'Mari sent me cause a my dream, Miss Red," Iona managed to yank her voice from some lost, locked cedar chest inside herself. "See, I dreamed of some monster and..."

"I know," Red replied. "I know the dream, and I know who sent it to you."

Iona sat in her favorite spot near the fire place on the stool that Red had made years ago just for her. She watched as the woman gently began removing the jars from the shelves. The liquid seemed to jump at the mere impression of Red's warmth against the glass. Iona thought that just maybe she had imagined this. Once in Red's hands, the liquid turned slow motions flips in the jar as if boiling with no heat. One by one Red poured jars into a huge tub slowly filling it. Bubbles bounced and jerked against one another and the sides of the tub without a single drop splattering. A deep sea of crimson grew anxiously awaiting the ceremony.

All this confounded Iona. Red usually showered her arrival with sugar kisses and honey dripping hugs, but now she busied herself about the house inattentive to the youth's presence. After numerous trips to and fro and the tub filled, Red stepped carefully toward Iona. Kneeling before her, Red's slender, willowy fingers and sandpaper palms caressed the child's quivering cheeks. This time she murmured, the raspiness hardly there, "It's time."

Iona followed the tender tug of Red's hand and beheld herself in the mirror wondering why the reflection betrayed her. A young woman stared back. Ceremoniously, methodically with lowered head and eyes, Red removed the young one's clothing. Piece by piece, she discarded them leaving time for Iona to search the foreign reflection desperately for some semblance of herself. She did not feel naked or ashamed before her own gaze or before Red. The smells, the love coiled themselves about her as Red loosed the thick, nappy tresses about her head.

"This," Red whispered curling her fingers through the pitch black strands about Iona's head, "this is a source of your strength. Braided it connects you to the belly of the earth and all its children. Loose, it calls upon the powers of the sky and wind. Cover it only when you need to be protected, but always, always wear it proudly."

Shyly Iona smiled as Red arranged the fluffy tufts of hair. For the first time, she did not view her hair an ugly, knotty inconvenience. She closed her eyes and imagined herself a princess with the most beautiful crown in the world.

With a fiery open palm, Red passed her hand from the crown of Iona's head to just above her closed eyes. "Here lies your link to the spirits, your ancestors, and your Creator. This shall cradle and guard your wisdom. Know the difference between your dreams and visions."

Slowly she opened her eyes to focus on the mirror. She recognized the peaceful, but strong face in the mirror as the same woman who appeared in her dreams more than 5 years before.

"Now you know her." Red responded, reading the young one's thoughts. "She has been waiting for you as you have grown to know and see her. You now wear your eyes open to the unseen." As Red turned slowly away, Iona saw the woman mysteriously aging right before her, aging with that same secret smile.

This time Red need not say a word. Iona gracefully ambled toward her and eased herself into the tub. The liquid, uncomfortably warm, lapped, and even pranced about Iona's body as her eyes widened in amazement but never fear. When Red stepped away, a rushing tide arose urgently slapping Iona's body pulling her beneath its waves.

A guide appears; she does not know who. Slowly the two descend into a dim, dank, earthen corridor. The area narrows. She finds herself alone. With eyes barely adjusting, she sees the corridor is just wide enough, tall enough, warm enough for her to fit. She hears them calling, crying, humming, moaning, shrieking occasionally. Their smells remind her of Red's house but now to the point of stench. Some speak in languages she does not understand, though in familiar tongues. Lying horizontally in what may be graves, layered at least 4 high on both sides, the voices draw her to their hands. Each one, sometimes with shredded fingers, sometimes with nothing but bone, lays hands on her, healing hands. They have long awaited her arrival, need her touch as much as need to touch her. She is their life-line and lingering hope for the true healing. Hypnotized her eyes fall upon each one who engraves himself/ herself into her spirit's eyes. Ascending gradually towards the light, she remembers only what is needed for the moment. The rest will come in time.

With her heaving chest slowing its rhythm to normal, Iona opened her eyes to blinding light, strange humming and the touch of Red's rough palms stroking her hand. Her eyes now clear fell upon Red's. The old woman's eyes were cloudy, very cloudy, and Iona wondered if she could even see. Infinite lines were softly etched on her hands, arms, everywhere. A muddy pool of soft ripples filled her face, beneath a cloud of foam-white, hair. Red's hair no longer moved, even when she herself did. She smiled that secret smile and spoke with much effort, "We must work while there is still time."

Again Iona stood before the mirror as Red smeared and massaged a heavy oil all over her glistening body. Her skin once mahogany glowed with scarlet tones. "This will seal the blood," said Red puffing and blowing. "It has always been about the blood, you know. Always. For centuries, our blood has been spilled violently about this earth even in our true land of birth. They spilled it, spilled it carelessly like throwing out God's garbage. Spilled it!" Iona heard Red raise her voice in quiet but fierce anger. "With every lick of a whip, every knife's slit, with all the bloody tears in a mother's torn eyes as her baby was snatched from the suckling of her breast—that blood was carelessly spilled!!! But it did not die! It cried. Cried seeing bodies dangling from trees, cried from violent seeds wrenching wombs, cried from the depths of the many graves at sea. Blood spilled before its time ain't blessed with death. Worse than any of us ever dared to dream, it cries from the bowels of the earth and stings the ears of the wind making its children hear. It cries and makes itself known to us even when time has forgotten. Before the dandelions peep their heads through the soil's skin, the blood springs up. And before the waters ruffle their waves, the blood laps the land with its fire. It cries and makes itself known!

Pausing to catch her breath, Red lowered her voice, "You, Iona, like I, are called to wipe up the blood. Wherever the blood has been spilled, it will scream your name now until it is lovingly soothed, cradled in your hands and placed to rest. It must be handled with the tenderest of care. Dab it gently with the suede from lambs' skins. Wring it carefully in sparkling clean jars. It must be saved, saved as memory, as wisdom, as warning for our generations to come. Saved as celebration for when no blood is left to scream and moan and cry." Red sank into a nearby chair. Slowly the trembling of her body stilled.

Gradually that secret smile again danced across the old woman's lips as a distance grew in her cloudy eyes, "Our children's children's children shall see and hear the blood singing! These children finally will laugh a laughter we shall never know. Dance in it! We laugh chile to survive. They shall laugh for the simple love of laughter itself."

Red now kneeled before Iona's taut frame firmly massaging the oil in her feet. Weeping with cracks and stubborn knots, Red's grip made Iona's entire body ache with their strength. Finishing the labor of love with a kiss to both the young feet, exhaustion consumed the old woman as her body poured itself into the floor.

Lessons learned, healing hymns, and slow dragging cups of strong tea filled the next days as the two women passed love, life and laughter between one another. They arose each morning hand stepping and foot clapping until the sun itself awoke. They toiled tirelessly until the day's end.

During their last hours together, night ran screeching form the whipping of a crude cutting wind and pelting tears of a frenzied sky. Folks could not recall a July night so cold. Lightning pranced mockingly as thunder ripped each heart. In his usually cozy one room, Mr. Lewis, like the rest of the elders, prayerfully braved the night. It was time.

The two women marched up the hill, undaunted by the furious storm, their faces pointed skyward. The old woman stumbled as the bullets of rain pelted her stubborn joints. With a feathery swoop, Iona caught her away from the earth's clutch. She carried the wilting woman as she would her first newborn, feeling Red's body deflate while filling her own.

At the hill's peak, she rested Red upon her feet. Beneath the kiss of the moon, her crown aglitter and skin aglow from the blood bath, Red passed the secrets of her smile to Iona. This time Iona removed Red's clothing and massaged her fragile body with the thick oil. While laboring she read the map of the old woman's body. Time and its wounds had printed their pathways across every inch of Red's decrepit frame. Iona read the footprints on her empty breasts, the tracks across her sagging cheeks, and the whispers along her wilted thighs. Drizzling her very last tears, Iona soothingly kissed the old woman's rheumatic crumpled feet.

Never looking back, Iona trudged away from the hilltop clutching swollen pieces of her heart, passing spirits on their way to meet the newest arrival. For the last time, Red smiled her secret smile as rain danced with the thin trickles of blood seeping from the corners of her wrinkled mouth and the soft folds burying eyes.

†

"Good morning, Miss Iona." The storekeeper flirted, his tongue slithering about the room as his eyes undressed the compelling woman before him.

Snatching his words and pitching them back in a crumpled, paper bag, Iona smiled her secret smile, "Why, good morning to you too, Edward." Edward's sweaty palms roamed and fumbled along the counter with everything he could get his hands on except Iona.

No one knew how old Iona was and couldn't remember her not being there. Nonetheless, they paid her the respect due to those old enough to name dirt. Her many years lied sleeping behind the still smooth, firm softness of her mahogany skin tinged with redwood, her silver laced, ebony tresses danced about her head .

"What can I help you with today?" the storekeeper asked knowing he would never hear the response he so lustfully desired.

"I need plenty jars, Edward, any kind of jars you got. Make sure that they are sparkling clean with lids tight fitting. I also need soft lamb skin, the newest you got. And by the way, has that big tub I ordered come in yet?"

HUSH

"Hush! Hush! Somebody's calling my name."

Beyond a shadow of a doubt, that must have been their absolute favorite song. Why they had to have been the most hand patting, foot tapping, juke jointing, rump rumbling, butt bumping, holy rolling, tambourine thumping, tongue talking, rip roaring, testifying, congregation this side of the entire Mississippi, I had ever heard in my life!

That's precisely why I decided to place my membership there. I needed to find out what was going on. They had the nerve to call themselves African First Church. Why they weren't even missionary Baptist! I didn't care that much though because door-to-dooring had never been my thing. Besides I really didn't have the time or patience for it.

Before the little storefront corner became African First, it had been known as Greater Mount Olive of Galilee. Too lazy to consult my Bible in those days, I wondered if Mount Olive were really in Galilee and if this church were truly any "greater" than the ones before it. But I couldn't half pronounce all them names of places I'd never been and would surely never go (in this life anyway), so I wasn't about to challenge anybody else's biblical knowledge.

Greater Mount Olive had been a tiny church that never made too much noise at all except beneath whispered breaths and behind half closed eyes, along a telephone line, in a barber or beauty shop, or after an uneventful prayer meeting where gossip grew the best. To have a peaceful, sacred name like Dove, the pastor raised more hell than many could imagine. Rev. Dove, a butt hungry, wrinkled, old coot, seemed to have a tremendous talent for seeking out the ailments of his distressed members.

From way atop that pulpit, it seemed as though he could see deep into their souls and know precisely when a marriage was failing, a spouse had been unfaithful, or even when folks were just plain bored with their lives. He knew instinctively that timing was important, so he'd wait until they were just about to fall apart at the seams or crack from the pressure or maybe melt into butter and sure enough he'd be right there to pick up the pieces, mend the cracks, and lick that butter. Believe it or not, the man resembled some kind of animal in the face and not a cute, cuddly one either. He looked like a cross between a bear, bulldog and I believe that animal in another country called "kwalla" or something. And he had the nerve to be old! That's what I couldn't understand. Who would want some <u>old</u> man, even if he were a preacher? What could he <u>possibly</u> do for somebody?

I finally figured that it was that timing of his, reaching for folks at their lowest, truly lowest point, that and the fact that he was a man of power being the head of a congregation and all. Not many black folk could boast of a position where they were actually running or controlling something outside of their own lives or the lives of their families (if they were indeed doing that). Times were hard for everybody then as they had always been. Seeing a man that ran things, that took charge with some semblance of confidence and dignity (even if only half way right) gave folks hope, made them feel good, and sometimes made them surrender. Besides all that, Rev. Dove could preach. From his holy helm, he could make them forget their troubles if only for a minute.

After a long, long history of having his own way, old, pug-nosed Dove, Rev. Dove, finally began to slip a bit in his old age. His timing was off. He no longer caught folks at their most vulnerable moments and just grabbed after them any moment he could. He even began soliciting "favors" from the wrong people. I remember him hobbling up to me once. With that lead limp of his, he still could manage to slide his slimy self up to somebody. He asked me about service that morning, if I enjoyed it. By the time he got to talking about "feeling the fire," he had managed to ease his silly self up to me and push his hand from my shoulder to the side of my breast while he tried to press that raggedy sack of chittlin's between his legs into my hip bone (like I was honestly supposed to feel something).

"Rev. Dove," I said, just a huffing, trying to remember the respect my folks had taught me to always have for my elders, "if you ever get this close to me and lay your hands on me again, I will momentarily risk losing my soul to the devil just long enough to haul off and smack the shit out of you. Do you understand?" Excuse my language, but those were my "hey days," you understand. Regaining the poise and patience of my little bit of religion, I then smiled right politely and added, "Now you have yourself a real nice afternoon."

After stooping to pick his face and that sad sack of spoiled chittlin's off the floor, he wobbled away without a word and never so much as looked me in the eyes again though he always managed to steal a glimpse of my behind. I could always tell when he did it, and it felt right nasty. I figured he just couldn't help himself as long as he didn't touch me again.

Shortly after that, Rev. Dove began drowning in a cesspool murky from his carelessness. He began soliciting the tender affections of teenaged girls and boys who he called in for special "counseling." Some of the young girls became pregnant and dragged themselves to the altar and begged for forgiveness. Pardoned by the mothers and deacons who each dried their tears and laid hands on them and prayed, they were "restored" to good standing in the church. I pitied those young girls wet with shame which no doubt affected in some negative way the babies they carried. My pity was mild, however, compared to my disgust watching the restoration ritual.

Those doing all the forgiving were often the keepers of some of the biggest mess going on in the church. Why just 2 months prior during their monthly fishing trip, Deacon Crawford and his sanctified drinking buddies had run his '67 convertible off the road and into the creek. Now you tell me what business does an old church deacon have with a convertible, let alone alcohol excess? In a panic, the men commenced to hollering and fighting one another to get the doors open which of course wouldn't budge due to the water pressure. No one seemed to notice that they were in a convertible with the top down. Suddenly Big Bertha Mae Tolliver, with her loud self, yelled from the other side of the creek, "Jump over the side, fools!" Somebody who saw the incident called the police. The officers who sought to charge Deacon Crawford for reckless and drunk driving had to tie him down and pump a pot of coffee down his throat before he could begin to comprehend his rights.

And don't get me started about the church Mothers. Sweet Mother Briscoe made her rounds all about town in her juke joint era. Even while on the Mother's board, she was known to satisfy several of the deacons as well as Pastor Dove himself until he got tired of her. That's the reason why none of the other Mother's cared for her especially our first lady, Sister Dove. I remember one time after service when the two of them fell out fighting and rolled down the center aisle with fist and hair and skirts just a flapping. Of course, that was talked about for the entire year by grown folks and children alike.

Besides all of that, I never saw a single young man accompany a one of those scared, young girls who had thrust herself into womanhood much too soon. Members finally admitted the possibility that at least one or two of these babies could have belonged to Rev. Dove. The young girls, however, refused to confess his involvement. Strangely , even after being restored, they cried often in church; many soon left the church all together.

Rev. Dove finally exhausted the patience of his members when he began approaching men in the church for "favors." Without the slightest hesitation, these men masterminded Rev. Dove's exile from his beloved Greater Mount Olive of Galilee. Old Dove, as they now called him, many feared that he had gone senile or just plain crazy. They felt sorry for him. Me, myself, I felt no sympathy for the old man but wished him comfort in the remaining years of his life. Nonetheless, anger grated on my nerves for no one ever took the charges and complaints against him seriously when only women and children were the victims. Only when the men complained did the congregation warrant any necessary action.

With the corruption and removal of their leader, the members of Greater Mount Olive bickered and wounded one another hopelessly. Many moved their memberships until the church dwindled down to nothing and finally disbanded. The lifeless storefront stood vacant and lonely for many a year until African First.

"Hush! Hush! Somebody's calling my name.'

Shango ushered himself and his merry band into town with little or no fanfare at all. They settled themselves quickly into the little store front and carried on services seven days a week. With such a tiny membership, folks were hardly interested at first, but a few of us decided to check out the happenings. With all the buzz about, visitors filtered in Sunday after Sunday to see if the new preacher was really "a man of God" (as if they honestly had some academic or scientific notion of how to figure such out). Many would leave abruptly in disgust after they noticed that the monumental portrait of Jesus that had always watched over Greater Mount Olive of Galilee had been replaced. I often imagined that Jesus would reach down one day and just stomp on old Dove with his ornery self standing up in the pulpit.

Shango had taken that picture of the golden, silky-haired, kind-eyed, pale-faced Jesus (who didn't look like anybody that ever set foot in that church) down and replaced it with the picture of a colored man or black man as Shango would say. This man, dressed in colorful robes, with deep maple skin and pitch black peering eyes above high, sharp cheek bones and a nose a mile wide, had had a halo of the nappiest hair I had ever seen. Now why the Almighty in his infinite wisdom would create a nappy-headed Savior like that, I don't know. Can you imagine Mary whipping that head every morning for 10 years? No wonder Joseph didn't want to claim Him before that angel laid the law down. I'm sure none of the other children in Bethlehem looked like this. More than anybody, this jungle Jesus looked more like Elroy McGinnis the notorious town drunk and beggar who was also an excellent handyman on the few occasions that he was sober.

Many of the visiting members, curious like I said, would waltz in and run up on that colored Jesus and turn right back around and hit the door. How dare that heathen, Shango, mock God and everything they had been taught to believe all of their lives! Elroy McGinnis, however, really didn't seem to be bothered at all by the hoopla. As a matter of fact, after backsliding for years off the ripple of that wine, he had the nerve to start coming to church every Sunday. I don't know if he ever heard a word Shango said or what the choir sang. He sat their puffed up in a trance admiring that picture like he was wondering what he would do if he were Jesus.

African First Baptist Church solidified its distance from the rest of the religious community in a number of ways. First of all, like I said when I started telling this story, they were a juke jointing church. The choir (often robed in African prints with many bright colors that some of them dark people had absolutely no business wearing) couldn't settle on the sanctity of a piano and organ with an occasional tambourine. Why they commenced to hootin' and hollerin' with the accompaniment of drums, *African drums*, base guitars, saxophones, shaking gourds, cymbals and anything else that would make noise. "If these hold their peace," Shango would bellow, " the rocks shall cry out." Frankly, I'm surprised the rocks didn't. You would think that rocks from all over the countryside and beyond would just tumble into town at any minute and hold themselves a holy roller convention right on the corner of African First. The members rumbled and rocked and shouted so in that church until if you passed by at the right time and looked hard enough, you could see the whole building sway slightly from side to side with the music. I kid you not! Once in a while, a members would burst through the doors shouting and carrying on something fierce. A few members or so even broken through the store front window and the stained glass on the sides. Ushers would come racing behind them with fans and handkerchiefs. Did they really think that could water the burning of the Spirit?

I joined African First at first out of curiosity so that I would have something to report back to the ladies meeting in town each week. Soon I began to enjoy myself and figured that the good Lord himself, or "Creator" as Shango called him, probably looked in on African First to have Himself a good time. So why shouldn't I? What with all the troubles of the world, God needed to shout and laugh, dance a little (holy dance, that is) and enjoy Himself too.

Attending African First was always a sight to see. Not only were choir members colorfully adorned, but every member on the Mothers Board wore her head wrapped or covered, sometimes in colored cloths, sometimes with big, beautiful hats sitting acey ducey. Shango mandated that these Mothers crown their heads to command a respect for their age and wisdom and work in the community. Members of the deacon board hustled about the church in colors of their choice and wore printed bands (sometimes with tassels) about their necks and shoulders that often matched the colored cloth of the women's head pieces. Members of both organizations were held in the highest esteem in the church. Their opinions were solicited and trusted wholeheartedly though each member was cautioned to "serve the Creator for himself" and know the boundaries and requirements of his own "Creation Contract" (an exclusive personal agreement and communication between a man or woman and his or her God).

Unlike most churches that I had attended, the choir was not divided into groups according to age. Everybody, who felt that he or she was called, sang with the choir from the tiniest who could barely talk to the oldest that could barely walk. No one seemed to mind how loud or soft, fast or slow, old school or new school the music. They all sang and praised together. Sometimes the music would linger. Children and babies would roam about freely often falling asleep in the aisle. Someone was always handy to look after them.

African First had the usual Wednesday night worship and prayer service and night service on Sunday evenings, but they always did things in their own way. They never attended the conventions or programs of other churches and never were really invited in the first place. Rarely was a member ever sick, and I don't recall anybody dying. Babies came several a year, and Shango spoke often of being grateful for the new souls that had joined us.

Children and elders were first in line at African First. All kinds of programs were set up in the church to meet their needs. Youth activities for all ages were plentiful with after school going- on, day care and special courses that lasted all year long. Parents came and often participated with their children. The programs for the elderly were service oriented. Meal programs, outings, field trips, exercise classes, and games took place all the time. At any event, the elders took "special seats" near the front and were personally escorted. No church affair concluded without parting words of wisdom or storytelling and testifying from at least one of the elders.

Young adults, single and married, with children and childless, took classes at various times during the week. As "the bridge between the young and old, birth and death," they were the hardest workers and organizers and hardly seemed to have time to grumble or gossip. I missed the gossip at first but quickly got used to not having any and finally didn't seem to even care. We all grew to know one another's names, one another's histories, families, likes and dislikes. Disagreements, arguments even a fight or two would break out as normal, but laughter and love eased all wounds and erased memories before their grudging time. After all members of African First simply had too much work to do to tarry .

I soon had no time for ladies meetings in town and grew very tired of "Girl, what's going on at that militant church of yours?" I no longer wanted to hear the bickering and debate, "How dare they call themselves 'African' first? Ain't they just plain niggers like anybody else?" I had no time to pay them/that any mind. I had found a community, a family that suited the needs of my own family amidst a world that could be cruel and uncaring. Colored children, thrust into the anger and hate of a black and white world, needed special arms to hold them, rock them to sleep, make them rise in the morning with dreams on their breath while giving them vision to birth those dreams. At African First, I felt at home. Anybody who questioned that could no longer fit comfortably in my life.

Shango often spoke of the great day when African First souls would have to "leave this place." "Brothers and sisters," he'd always begin in that same way, "Our ancestors have bled and died awfully painful deaths so that we might have the opportunities that we have this day. Contrary to what much of history prepares us to believe, the black man resisted the chains of bondage long before Malcolm and Martin, long before Frederick Douglas, long before Harriet Tubman, Sojourner Truth, and the many, many others.

"Black men and women and children began resisting the chains of bondage even before their journey across the Middle Passage. Some threw their chains to the waves in resistance and drowned in the blessed peace of the waters. Others fed their very own flesh to the treacherous jaws of sharks circling before the ship. Still others crossed that Passage, and upon reaching these shores, they revolted. Remembering the many tortured with sickness, starvation and cruelty, recalling the ceaseless cries of their loved ones and foreseeing the suffering yet to come for their children and future generations, they gathered their loved ones and all those chains, and with souls searing in angst again they stepped off the boat.

"Refusing death in the waters this time, they began to just walk on the ocean. The cries from the many graves murmuring beneath the waters rose up under their feet and formed a pathway leading to the air. And they kept on walking until the pain and anguish in their bodies began to take root and sprout wings. Can't you see them?

"Breaking loose from their shackles and casting away their chains, their wings cut the wind, and they suddenly began to fly. Without pain and regrets, they flew away; without fear in their hearts, they flew away. Without worry of where they might land or how they would feed their children or concern of what anybody else thought they just kept on flying away. Leaving whispers in the air for us to hear and revere this very day, they flew away!"

These words sprang from tears, shouts of joy and faraway eyes. Finally, Shango settled back into himself. His voice softened, "Let us not forget to honor those who chose to stay in this place and plant the seeds that we might be here at this very moment. Though we still suffer from time to time, we are a resilient people rebounding from one terror to another. And so we remain but only for a short while longer, children. African First has now sown its own seeds and done the deeds of the Creator's calling. With our knees rooted in the earth from centuries of service, the harvest awaits us. We won't stay 'round here much longer."

In the great way of colored folk, black people, the rhythm had taken over by this time and words were needed no longer. Rhythms ripped across the organ, clipped the treble of the ivories, boomed in the belly of the base and then screamed through the agony of the saxophone. Even the tongues of tambourines shouted as the drums (both visible and invisible) had their way all about the church. Young and old alike step danced in the aisles, about the pulpit and all through the choir stand. No one but me seemed to notice when one of the pews fell back and slammed against the floor with not a soul injured. Fans flew up in the air and handkerchiefs darted about. By this time, I could no longer hold my own peace and remember nothing thereafter but the closing hymn...

"Hush! Hush! Somebody's calling my name."

My family and I just happened to miss that last Sunday. We had been out of town to see my husband's people. His father, a very ill man, had requested that we bring the children up to see him while he was yet in his right mind. Tired from the long journey home, I awoke the next morning with that song turning over and over in my mind. I roamed the house and checked on the children and decided to let them sleep a little longer. I considered going to worship by myself that morning but settled instead on a cup of hot coffee in the rare silence of the house for a couple of hours.

Early the next morning, I headed off to the church because I was on the special committee for the annual ceremony honoring our eldest members. Astonished I approached the little corner to see no hustling and bustling about and not even a light inside. The door unlocked, I figured someone had to leave and would come right back. I entered the sanctuary to find a hazy film of I don't know what hanging in the air. Colorful robes with their shells, lace dresses with matching hats, suits and ties, shoes and sox, canes and walkers, strollers and umbrellas lay lifeless all about the altar, aisles and pews. Even the one suit that Elroy McGinnis owned was sprawled in his regular place on the pew.

Heart heavy, I turned and left that old storefront church on its corner. Though asked a hundred questions and interviewed several times, I never told a soul. Who would believe me anyway? The newspapers said that it was a distasteful joke, a dirty trick that the congregation had played "knowing they were not wanted in this town." I knew better and only wished that I and my family had attended service that day.

Years have passed since African First's homegoing. From time to time, I just take my time and linger at that corner. Sometimes when I am there by myself and the streets are right quiet, the building seems to rock just slightly from side to side, and I am comforted as I hear echoes of the souls singing, "Hush! Hush! Somebody's calling my name." And I work and laugh and work and wait for my own name to be called.

Amen

BURNT BOTTOM

Weary from a tedious day's toil, the crinkles of Nadine's lined eyes had just ceased their nervous trembling and settled into a sea of sweet dreams. Bang! Nadine's entire body flinched with an all too familiar tension as the screen door slammed after Booker's footsteps resounding throughout the house. Five years and he still made her heart jump high enough to reach that soft spot in the center of her throat, the same soft spot that was just one of his favorites.

She lied on her side, back towards him motionless except for a faint smile. She heard the growl of his zipper and the gentle wash of his pants down those smooth, thick legs. She even knew the sound of his shirt rustling the coarse, satiny curls atop his head. Quietly he lifted the covers. The cool air fluttered about Nadine's back and shoulders beneath the worn flannel gown. Daring to touch the rest of her body, the tip of Booker's nose barely nuzzled the nape of her neck scattered with beckoning strands of hair. Pretending sleep, Nadine clutched her breath, clenched her eyes and tried to still the waves wavering between her hips as the tip of Booker's nose made its way around to trail the lobe of her ear and dip barely inside of it.

Soliciting her passions, Booker slid his hands along the textured gown exposing a glowing, round shoulder. A muddy moan, conceived in Nadine's toes, crawled helplessly to her ankles, slid about the curve of her calves, swelled to fill the plump pockets of her knees, and bubbled all about her thighs. That muddy moan then mumbled to her womb as Booker's commanded her flesh. His palms eventually met that moan and kneaded it into thinning honey hushes that would hold no longer as Nadine rolled over with the burning tide of her passion and swallowed Booker's lips between her own...

Tonight his taste was foreign to her, not the usual flavor of expensive liquors mingling with the natural sweetness of his breath. This taste was acrid, like dry, scorching flames. By now his hands had succeeded in removing her gown and traveled skillfully exploring her body. Somehow through these hot hands, something icy and sharp poked and prodded Nadine causing her body to shudder.

Not wanting to destroy the mood, she reached for his hands and cuddled their warmth against the coolness of her cheek and kissed them while searching, finding only the same smooth, masculine softness without a callous or scar. Mannishly Booker rolled his body onto hers and groaned as he felt her breasts inflate against his chest. His lips grazed the soft hollow at the center of her neck teasing with a flicker from his sweating tongue, but the ripple in her womb ceased as a glacial sheet draped itself slowly about her body. Growing mysteriously numb, she lied baffled and petrified as frost formed along the bedroom walls.

Desperately embracing his warmth for answers, Nadine lied motionless as Booker's arms enclosed her. Pressure pumped and pushed inside her skull as her vision blurred and breath lessened. Booker, unconscious of her discomfort, slid himself inside of her gently and steadily, patiently and passionately as always. His presence, usually welcomed, was abrasive as frosted splinters seemed to nestle themselves about her insides. Wicked laughter riveted from the base of her skull to the tip of her tail bone, from every nook and cranny of the spinning room, and even from beneath the rocking bed. Gradually Nadine's numbness disappeared as the laughter echoed, frost melted, prodding and poking ceased, and the foreign smells drifted away. Her numbness, accompanied by bruises, lay smothered in bloody sheets. Dripping with perspiration that was not her own, she opened her eyes to glimpse a sudden, dark, long-haired, shapely shadow flying from the room. The laughter, the odor, the glass splinters, the frost were not hers. They belonged to the other woman Booker wore home that night.

"Damn it!" he raged. "Why didn't you tell me?" Making love to a woman during her moon scared Booker more than it disgusted him. Nadine replied simply by rising and gliding slowly to the bathroom, slowly enough to allow him to see the mess, the filth that he had made, he and that other woman. Her period would not arrive for another 15 days, faithful as always, unlike her husband. She had never said a word to Booker about his promiscuity and unfaithfulness before, so no need to say it now. She had always known who and what he was well before she married him.

†

"I'm gonna make you **my** woman," he had boasted emphasizing the word "my" as if it had really meant something while Nadine pretended not to hear. This dinner date was her very first with Booker and perhaps the only chance she'd have to hook him.

"Girl, I know you stuck your foot in that pie, 'cause it's mighty good to me," he grinned dabbing dribbles of her peach cobbler from the corners of his full lips.

"I ain't your girl," she sassed, "and everything good to you ain't always good for you, Booker T. Lee," she added ignoring the wit of her own words while concealing the giggles waiting to explode from the back of her throat.

"That's why I likes you, woman," he shot back as a stealthy arm crept about her waist for the first time, lingering at the small of her back. "I likes you for that mouth of yours and for the bottom of them pots."

"You fool! What do pots got to do with it?" she asked between the leaks of giggles now spilling from her belly.

"My mama taught me a woman with 'burnt bottom pots' make you a good wife. 'Burnt bottom' means they thick-laced with love." Booker christened these words with a stolen first kiss as Nadine's bones disintegrated and the rest of her remained only to be swept up from the floor. She had surrendered herself to the one man practically every woman wanted and the one man almost every woman could certainly have.

†

Booker T. Lee was the kind of man that would just melt in your mouth when you touched your tongue to him. He was a man's man simply because he was a ladies' man first. Men folk called him "Doc T. Lee" and said he had seen more nookie than a gynecologist on a full moon. Women for miles around delighted in handling a piece of him, rather him handling a piece of them if only for a moment. Those who had sampled his wares testified that his magical jade stick was not dipped in gold but powdered in fine gold dust with tiny pearls, fresh from the oyster, lining its ridge. From the feathery skin of his scalp to the sacred soft leather of his feet, taut, velvety smooth, walnut skin wrapped itself about his bulging, muscular frame as if hugging some precious gift. Something on his body always beckoned even in his sleep: a wisp of hair waving, a finger tapping, a thigh muscle solo dancing. Something always beckoned not nervously or in irritation, but just like he was ever ready. Booker never had to say much or even ask for it. His silken eyes and satin smile, fluent in the most lustful tongues, barely flashed and women just fell at his feet.

A man's gotta do what a man's gotta do...

... And Booker certainly did. Booker passed his kisses 'round whimsically believing that he possessed an endless supply. He hailed himself as a blessing to the many women without men and even to the ones with men who needed that extra helping hand, hug or hump to get them through the night or day. Why Nadine should simply consider it her sister/womanly duty to share the joy and beauty that he had brought to her life! Why go to the doctor, drugstore, church, school or shrink when Booker could supply their needs, for free? Besides if Eve had gone to Adam instead of to that damn snake, the world would be in much better shape. So Booker passed his kisses 'round unconcerned with the consequences passed back to him.

Nadine never minded the phone calls constantly hanging up as she answered, the snide remarks sashaying behind her back, or the gossip romping both about and beyond town about her husband. All she wanted and needed was that he be the man she married-- kind, gentle, loving, gorgeous and hard working. The rest she could care less about as long as he paid her and their home the respect of not having to deal with any mess. Mess. She couldn't stand mess, dust, dirt, filth, unclean spirits, soiled souls or unsanitary habits. To date, Booker had always come to her clean no matter where he had been or what he'd been doing while there. He had always come to her clean that is until he staggered upon the wrong woman.

With monkeys making merry on his back, Booker never seemed to understand that the passing of flesh between two people included the contact of spirits abiding about them. Monkeys on the back naturally multiplied when screwing other monkeys. This last woman, however, packed more than monkeys. Panthers purred between her legs. Lizards dangled from the hardened lobes of her ears. Snakes slithered about her neck and breasts, and a jackal rested on her shoulder. So Booker's monkeys, unprepared for this particular jaunt in the jungle, made the serious mistake of bringing mess home.

A man's gotta do what a man's gotta do, but a woman got to be herself somehow...

The night of the brutal beating, Nadine began cleaning that mess by soaking in the tub for hours. Monotonously she massaged, then scrubbed, then massaged again heeding the bruises and dried blood about her body. She stared at the water dense and murky with stains. Tears and pain flowed down the drain with her sorrow. After scouring the tub, she drew fresh water, tossed in healing, aromatic salts and repeated the ritual three times. Finally dressed with her skin achingly clean and water wrinkled, she waltzed past Booker never even noticing him or his curious eyes. The screen door slammed after her this time in the middle of the night leaving Booker haunted by her silence and the wretched echoes of that other woman's laughter.

After spending the night cuddling up to the comfort of the river bank beneath the star's kisses and whispering wisdom of the moon, Nadine returned home that next morning well after Booker had gone to work only to find drawers disheveled with clothes spilling over, garbage strewn about the floor, furniture kicked and overturned, and both the kitchen and bathroom filled with filth. Them damn monkeys had made mess all about the rest of the house.

She began her cleaning in the bathroom by scrubbing the tub, toilet, faucets, sink and floor and sponging everything else with disinfectants and bleach. Moving throughout each room, she unhung all the curtains and soaked them in strong detergents and hot water baths ignoring what the labels suggested. She washed windows inside and out with a coat of ammonia polishing them until she could see herself. She then dusted, soaped, bathed and buffed all wooden frames, doors, floors and their baseboards. Grumbling spiders searched for safety as she conquered their cob webs and rinsed them down the drain. Sweat now simmering and cleansing her bones, Nadine packed the garbage and unwanted goods out the door to the back yard and built herself a fire.

With bandanna guarding her mouth and nose and doo rag protecting her head, Nadine summoned her courage for a shield and bravely marched up the stairs to the bedroom with an army of healing haints single filed behind her. She jerked the sheets, blankets, tick and pillows from the bed and pitched them out the window to feed to the bonfire below. As she stood now before the blaze, ashes soared in the air like glowing, black bats afire. She watched to insure that each piece burned and burned and burned thoroughly before the tears in her eyes as she gently tossed pictures of Booker to nourish the flames. The fire finished, she shoveled the glowing hot ashes and scooped them into a hand-painted urn.

Nadine heard the rattling of the front door as she entered from the back door but never flinched a muscle, never broke her stride, never even paused to glance at Booker. She had no time; she wasn't done cleaning the mess. Returning home from work much earlier than usual, Booker dragged about the house heavily avoiding her. Exhausted and feverish he cowardly tucked himself in bed before noon and couldn't have come out if he had wanted.

After several days of serving Booker his meals in bed and repeating the house cleaning ritual to her scrutinizing inspection, Nadine began cleaning the entire kitchen. With each room conquered, she had grown stronger washing away sorrowful memories and burdensome blemishes that she had carried for far too long. Not just Booker either, she had washed the mess from him and that other woman away a while ago. She no longer slept with him and rarely spoke or looked at him, not from anger or agony, but simply because she was busy, busy cleaning.

Cleaning and cooking were the two things that made her feel good, strong and in control these days, made her skin perspire and glow, made her muscles ache and smile filling the house with song. She felt privileged to be one of the very few colored women around who didn't have to work cleaning and cooking or anything for somebody else. To her great pleasure, she had only to work for herself and her husband, and she intended to keep it that way. Even with all that mess gone, she still remained a scrubbing junkie and knew this was a high that couldn't hurt her. Nadine baptized every appliance, dish, utensil, cupboard, cabinet and pantry in the place with righteousness. At last she settled to pots, pans and skillets.

"'Burnt bottoms'," she thought and smiled with sweet memories of Booker from years ago. "Well," she sighed somewhat sadly aloud to herself, "there'll be 'burnt bottoms' no more. Time has come for everything to be cleaned."

For days as Booker grew continually sick and coughed ferociously upstairs, Nadine labored with steel wool and scrapers and cleansers to make her pans and skillets brand spanking new again. Well before Booker told her, she had known that her pans and skillets were laced with love for they had belonged to her mother, given by her mother, and given by her mother well before her. That was the reason why of all the women around town, Booker fell for Nadine to make a wife; she wooed him with those love laced pots. She knew now that she was washing away centuries of love, history and memory that only these pots recalled. Nonetheless, she believed that if the love, the history, the memory really belonged to her, somehow they would remain. Perhaps they had already been soaked up in her fingertips, and the palms of her hands. "No need to worry," she soothed herself. "Love don't just wipe and wash away."

Upstairs the walls, the bed, the pillows, the covers seemed to grow cold and mutter once again all about Booker. He began hearing things from the cracks and corners of the room, especially when he started to touch his self. It was the one thing he could always count on when at a loss for words or in trouble or just plain bored. Now for some reason, it didn't seem to work anymore or amuse him. His self just lied there lifeless like he did. Eyes and cheeks puffed, head, nose and throat clogged, he could no longer speak and could hardly open his eyes. Daily his ashen body grew more pale and weak and blistered with bed sores. Turning his head on the pillow, he noticed dry tufts of hair.

Unable to move his stiff arms and legs, he felt a burning tear along his cheek as he thought of his last night of making love to "his woman." Of all the women he had ever laid hands on, Nadine loved him for simply who he was, not how he "performed." He wondered if she loved him now broken and helpless in all that mess he had made. If he could just make his self-work, perhaps it would change Nadine's behavior towards him. She wasn't cruel or nasty or even impolite, she just seemed to no longer pay him attention as if he were a piece of furniture or something.

"Done!" announced Nadine to herself proudly as she victoriously scrubbed the last stubborn specks from those "Burnt Bottoms" and placed them to soak in a tub of bleach and scalding hot water. Tip toeing up the stairs with Booker's dinner tray, she eased the bedroom door open. Startled her heart leapt and thudded against the soft hollow of her throat as Booker lay narrow eyes glassy with his neck and chin crusty from dried drool. Nadine gasped staring at her husband seeing him really for the first time in weeks. With one hand wrapped around his exposed self, the other clutching a picture of her, he had choked from the acid of his own vomit. She wondered to herself how long had he suffered and why hadn't he asked for help? Terribly preoccupied with her work, she honestly had not noticed how sick Booker had become, and he never even attempted to call it to her attention. For a second guilt shook her heart until she realized Booker had left another damn mess for her to clean.

†

The ceremony was elegant, intimate and simple with only immediate family and closest friends at the closed casket, grave side memorial. Far away all about the town, taverns mourned as Booker's female patrons poured their sorrows into hard liquor bottles while hungry wolves stood waiting to soothe and later devour them.

Alone at last at the grave site, Nadine opened the casket and gently stroked Booker's sagging, frozen cheek. She smiled approvingly. Upon her request, the mortician had finally managed to pry Booker's hands away from his self and Nadine's picture and replace them with an urn of strange, laughing ashes, and a tiny, "burnt bottom" pan.

ABOUT THE AUTHOR

Tamara J. Madison is an internationally traveled writer, poet, and performer currently living in Atlanta, Georgia. Her work has been published in various literary journals, magazines, and anthologies including *Poetry International*, *Tidal Basin Review*, *aaduna*, and *Black Magnolias*.

She is the author of *Collard County, A Collection of Short Stories*, and *Kentucky Curdled*, a poetry and essay collection and poetry audiobook. Her album, *Naked Voice*, is Grand Prize Winner of the First Literary Recording Contest for Manzanita Quarterly and AUTHENTIC VOICEwork Records and is an Editor's Pick on independent music distributor, CD Baby.

She has performed for stage and television as a solo and collaborative artist. She also facilitates creative expressions workshops for youths and adults.

Tamara is the publisher and editor of *TamTalk!!!*, a weekly newsletter of creative inspiration and motivation for fellow artists, writers, and "just plain folk."

To contact her or for more samples of her work, blog, audio and video, visit her home on the web at www.tamarajmadison.com.

NOTE TO THE READER

Want to know more about Collard County and its residents?

Curious about the origins of these stories and the author's inspiration?

*Start a discussion with me on Amazon or my home on the web!**

Share with a book club or other reading group!

Keep the discussion going, and support independent writers and artists!

Many thanks,

Tamara

*www.tamarajmadison.com